Within the fairy-tale treasury which has come into the world's possession, there is no doubt Hans Christian Andersen's stories are of outstanding character. Their symbolism is rich with character values. From his early childhood in the town of Odense, Denmark, until his death in Copenhagen, Hans Christian Andersen (1805-1875) wrote approximately 150 stories and tales. The thread in Andersen's stories is one of optimism which has given hope and inspiration to people all over the world. It is in this spirit that the Tales of Hans Christian Andersen are published.

THE BUCKWHEAT
by Hans Christian Andersen
Translated from the original Danish text by Hans Henrik
Breitenstein
Illustrated by Tiziana Gironi
U.S. Edition 1988 by WORD Inc., Waco. TX 76702
Text: © Copyright 1988 Scandinavia Publishing House,
Nørregade 32, DK-1165, Copenhagen K. Denmark
Artwork: © Copyright 1988 Tiziana Gironi and
Scandinavia Publishing House
Printed in Portugal
ISBN 0-8499-8549-8

Hans Christian Andersen
The Buckwheat

Illustrated by Tiziana Gironi
Translated from the original Danish text
by Hans Henrik Breitenstein

WORD INC.
Waco, TX 76796

Often, after a thunderstorm when one walks past a field of buckwheat, one notices that it looks quite black and burnt. It is as though a fire has gone over it. Then the farmer says, "The lightning did it." But why is it so? I will tell you what the gray sparrow told me. And the gray sparrow heard it told by an old willow tree which stood by a buckwheat field, and still stands there today.

4

It is a big and dignified willow tree, but old and full of wrinkles, and it has split down the middle where grass and brambles grow out of the crack. The tree leans to one side and the branches hang down to the ground, as if they were strands of long, green hair.

In the fields nearby grew corn, rye, barley and oats. Aye even the lovely oats grew there which, when they are ripe, look like a great number of little yellow canaries on a branch. The corn was blessedly fruitful, and the heavier the fruit, the lower it bowed in pious humility.

But then there was also a field of buckwheat, and this field was right beside the old willow tree.

The buckwheat did not bow down like the other corn. It stood straight, proud and stiff-necked.

"I am as rich as the ear," it said,
"and besides I am much prettier. My
flowers are more beautiful, like apple
blossoms. It delights the eye to look at
us. Do you know any as fair as us old
willow?"

And the willow nodded his head as if to say, "Indeed I do." But the buckwheat was so puffed up with pride, it said, "Silly old tree! It is so old that it has got grass growing in its belly."

9

10

Now a violent thunderstorm was
coming near. All the flowers of the
field folded up their crowns or bowed
their fine heads while the storm raged
overhead. But the buckwheat remained
stiff with pride.

"Bow your head, like we do," the flowers said.

"I do not need to do so," the buckwheat said.

"Bow your head, like we do," the corn shouted, "now the angel of the storm is on the wing. He has got wings that reach from the sky right down to the ground, and he will cut you up before you can beg his mercy."

"Aye, but I will not bow," the buckwheat replied.

14

15

"Close your flowers and bow your leaves," said the old willow tree. "Do not look towards the lightning when the heavens open. Even men dare not do so because in the lightning you can see into God's heaven, but this sight blinds even men. What might happen to us lowly growths of the earth if we dared do that, we who are far inferior."

17

"Far inferior?" said the buckwheat. "Now, that is exactly what I want, to look right into God's heaven."

And so it did, in arrogance and pride. It seemed as though the whole world was on fire, there were so many lightning bolts.

19

20

When the evil weather had passed,
the flowers and the corn stood in the
still, clean air, refreshed by the rain.
But the buckwheat had been burned
black as coal by the lightning, and was
now a dead, useless weed in the field.

And the old willow tree moved its branches in the wind, and great drops of water fell from the green leaves, as though the tree were crying. The sparrows asked, "Why are you crying, old willow?"

And the willow tree told them about the buckwheat's pride, arrogance and punishment; it always follows.

I, who tell the story, heard it from the sparrows. They told it to me the evening when I asked for a fairy tale.

The Buckwheat

Explaining the story:

The buckwheat considered itself more important than it really was. It was presumptuous and proud. It would not admit that others were more beautiful or wiser than itself. Instead of listening to the old willow tree, the corn and the flowers, the buckwheat arrogantly mocked them.

Talking about the truth of the story:

What does the old proverb mean, "Pride goes before a fall"?

Describe the old willow tree. What does **"and still stands there today"** mean?

What characterized the corn?

What did the flowers do when the storm came?

What does the storm angel symbolize?

When did the buckwheat's arrogance peak?

Applying the truth of the story:

Why is it so important to listen to those who are older and wiser than us?

How should we respond when the hard times come?